Ruminations of an Expatriate

Volume II
Reflections

By

Christopher Mark Brown

ABOUT THE AUTHOR

Christopher Mark Brown was the third of seven children, born in Olympia, Washington, the state's capital. His father later became an administrative assistant and speechwriter for Congresswoman Julia Butler Hansen, a role that moved the family to the suburbs of Washington, D.C. In a household where politics and world events were constant conversation, the evening news with Walter Cronkite and the unfolding tragedy of the Vietnam War shaped Christopher's early worldview.

By the late 1960s, as a young man searching for justice and meaning, Christopher became deeply involved in anti-war activism. At twenty, he described himself as a communist and joined the Venceremos Brigade, traveling to Cuba through Canada in solidarity with revolutionary movements abroad. These experiences, and the political atmosphere of his upbringing, ignited a lifelong passion for human rights, writing, and social commentary.

Christopher's path was not limited to activism. In Washington State he built a life rooted in the land, becoming an accomplished farmer near Elma and later serving his community as the town's public works director. His connection to the soil reflected a quieter side of a man who had once marched in the streets.

In the early 2000s, disillusioned with the direction of American politics during the administration of George W. Bush, Christopher chose a different path and retired to Mexico. There he continued writing, reflecting on politics, culture, and the experiences that had shaped his life.

A lover of folk music and a devoted guitarist, Christopher found joy in simple things: tending the land, playing songs, and sharing ideas. His blog became a lifeline, an ongoing conversation with friends, family, and readers, where his voice, curiosity, and convictions lived on.

Table of Contents

PART I: WHEN LIFE BECOMES NORMAL...................................1

    Chapter 1: The Second Year Begins 2

    Chapter 2: Settled, But Not Still...............................5

    Chapter 3: The Rhythm of Elsewhere 10

Part II THE UNRAVELING OF EXPECTATIONS 15

    Chapter 4: The Quiet Drift 16

    Chapter 5: The Myth of Simplicity 20

    Chapter 6: Living Without Edges................................24

PART III: RELATIONSHIPS WITHOUT ANCHORS 28

    Chapter 7: Distance Changes Everything.........................29

    Chapter 8: Infidelity Abroad 33

    Chapter 9: The Illusion of Reinvention 37

    Chapter 10: Intimacy Without Permanence 41

PART IV: THE EXPAT MICROCOSM.....................................45

    Chapter 11: A World of Transients..............................46

    Chapter 12: Conversations on Repeat 50

    Chapter 13: Watching Others Become Someone Else............54

PART V: MORAL DRIFT..59

    Chapter 14: Different Rules Apply Here.........................60

    Chapter 15: The Slippery Slope.................................64

    Chapter 16: Justifying Everything 68

PART VI: BETWEEN WORLDS..73

Chapter 17: Looking Back at Home...................................... 74

Chapter 18: The Myth of Stability.................................... 78

Chapter 19: Nowhere Feels Permanent 82

PART VII: RECKONING WITH THE SELF 87

Chapter 20: The Person You Become.................................... 88

Chapter 21: Freedom Revisited 92

Chapter 22: The Weight of Choice 97

Epilogue: No Final Answers.. 102

PART I:

WHEN LIFE BECOMES NORMAL

Chapter 1: The Second Year Begins

The second year doesn't announce itself.

There's no ceremony, no marker, no moment where you wake up and say, this is it, I live here now. It just arrives quietly, like a habit you didn't notice forming. One day you're still explaining yourself, why you came, how long you'll stay, and the next, you stop offering explanations altogether. Not because you have better answers, but because the questions feel less relevant.

The first year was defined by edges. Everything had them. Every experience was sharp, outlined, and new. Streets weren't just streets, they were foreign. Conversations weren't just conversations, they were negotiations across culture, language, expectation. Even the simplest tasks carried a sense of accomplishment, like you were earning your place one awkward interaction at a time.

But sometime between the last "first time" and the hundredth repetition, something shifted.

Life stopped feeling temporary.

Not in a dramatic way, there was no declaration, no conscious decision, but in the way routines began to anchor themselves. You stopped noticing the route to the grocery store. You stopped translating menus in your head. You stopped being surprised by the small inconveniences that once felt like proof you didn't belong. Instead, they became part of the background noise of daily life, no more remarkable than traffic or weather.

And that's when it happens, the subtle, almost unsettling realization:

You're no longer visiting.

You're living.

At first, this feels like progress. It's what you wanted, after all. The goal was never to remain an outsider forever, peering in from the edges of someone else's world. The goal was integration, however imperfect. To move through life without friction, without constantly being reminded that you are somewhere else.

And yet, with that ease comes something unexpected.

The loss of intensity.

The first year was exhausting, yes, but it was also vivid. Every day carried weight. Every interaction mattered. You were hyper-aware of yourself, your surroundings, your place in it all. There was a kind of accidental mindfulness to it, born not from discipline but from necessity. You had to pay attention, because nothing was automatic.

Now, things are automatic. You wake up, go through your routines, move through your day without thinking about every step. You blend in, not perfectly, but enough that you're no longer constantly observed, and more importantly, you're no longer constantly observing yourself.

And strangely, that's where a new kind of question begins to form.

If this is no longer temporary… then what is it?

The idea of "just passing through" had been a kind of safety net. It gave everything a provisional quality. Mistakes didn't matter as much. Choices didn't feel permanent. You could always leave, reset, return to some version of your life that existed before all of this.

But the second year erodes that illusion.

Because now you have patterns. You have relationships, not deep ones necessarily, but recurring ones. Familiar faces. Predictable rhythms. You've built something, even if you didn't mean to.

And anything that can be built… can also be stayed in.

That's the part no one really talks about when they romanticize expatriate life. The fantasy is always about movement, about escape, reinvention, freedom. But the reality, eventually, becomes stillness. Not the comfortable stillness of home, but a quieter, more ambiguous version of it. A stillness that asks: Are you going somewhere, or have you already arrived?

The second year doesn't feel like an adventure.

It feels like a life.

And that's both the achievement, and the problem.

Because once life becomes normal, you're no longer reacting to a place.

You're revealing who you are inside it.

Chapter 2: Settled, But Not Still

Comfort arrives the way dust does, gradually, quietly, without asking permission.

You don't notice it forming. Not at first. It gathers in the spaces where uncertainty used to live. In the routines you no longer question. In the streets you walk without thinking. In the small, almost invisible decisions that no longer require effort.

By the second year, life has become manageable.

You know where to go. You know how things work. You've built a version of daily life that functions, efficiently enough that you stop paying attention to it. The friction is gone, or at least reduced to something tolerable. You're no longer negotiating every moment.

And for a while, this feels like success.

Because it is.

You've crossed the threshold from outsider to participant. Maybe not fully, maybe not permanently, but enough that the distinction stops dominating your experience. You can exist here without constantly translating yourself. You can move through the day without feeling like you're performing it.

But comfort has a strange side effect.

It makes space.

And in that space, something else begins to surface.

At first, it's subtle, more of a feeling than a thought. A kind of low-level restlessness that doesn't have a clear source. You can't point to anything that's wrong. In fact, if you were asked directly, you'd probably say things are fine. Good, even. Life is stable. Predictable. Easier than it used to be.

So why does it feel like something is missing?

The problem isn't discomfort. It's the absence of it.

In the first year, everything demanded your attention. You were too occupied with figuring things out to question what it all meant. Survival, social, logistical, emotional, was enough of a focus to fill your days. There was no room for restlessness because there was no stillness.

Now there is.

And stillness has a way of amplifying whatever sits underneath it.

The days begin to blur, not in a dramatic or depressing way, but in a quiet, almost imperceptible flattening. One day resembles the next. Not exactly, but enough that they lose their sharpness. Time doesn't slow down or speed up, it just... evens out.

You wake up, move through your routines, interact with the same circles of people, return to the same spaces. Nothing is particularly wrong with any of it. But nothing feels particularly charged, either.

It's not boredom.

It's something more complicated than that.

Because boredom suggests you want something to do. This feels more like you're not sure what wanting would even look like here.

There's a kind of emotional neutrality that sets in. A leveling. Highs aren't as high, but lows aren't as low. You become steadier, but also, in a way, less vivid to yourself.

And that's when the question starts to shift.

In the beginning, it was: Can I live here?

Now it becomes: Do I want to?

Not as a dramatic ultimatum, but as a quiet, recurring thought that appears at unexpected moments. Walking home. Sitting in a café. Watching other people move through their lives with a kind of ease that still feels slightly out of reach.

It's not dissatisfaction with the place, exactly.

It's something more internal than that.

Because by now, you've learned an inconvenient truth: changing your environment doesn't change your underlying patterns. It just gives them new shapes to take.

The same tendencies follow you. The same questions. The same uncertainties about what you're doing, who you're becoming, what any of it is leading toward. They don't disappear just because the backdrop has changed. If anything, they become more visible once the external challenges fade.

And so you start to notice yourself again.

Not in the hyper-aware way of the first year, where everything felt exposed and uncertain, but in a quieter, more reflective way. You begin to observe your own routines. Your habits. The way you spend your time when no one is watching, when nothing is forcing your hand.

And sometimes, what you see isn't entirely reassuring.

You realize how much of your life has become default. Not chosen deliberately, but drifted into. The places you go. The people you see. Even the version of yourself you present, it all begins to feel less like a series of intentional decisions and more like momentum carrying you forward.

That's the unsettling part.

Not that anything is wrong, but that nothing is being actively decided.

You're settled.

But you're not still.

Because beneath the surface stability, there's movement, subtle, internal, difficult to define. A sense that something is shifting, even if you can't yet say what it is. A tension between the life you've built and the awareness that it might not be enough.

Or maybe it is enough, but not in the way you expected.

The second year doesn't bring clarity.

It brings contrast.

Between comfort and unease. Between routine and restlessness. Between the version of life you imagined and the one you're actually living.

And somewhere in that contrast, a new phase begins, not marked by external change, but by something quieter, more persistent:

The feeling that standing still might actually be a form of drifting.

Chapter 3: The Rhythm of Elsewhere

At some point, without noticing exactly when, life stops feeling foreign.

Not because the place has changed, but because you have.

The unfamiliar becomes familiar in increments so small they barely register. The sounds that once stood out dissolve into background noise. The patterns of the day, when people move, when they rest, when things open and close, stop feeling irregular and start to feel expected. You no longer measure everything against where you came from. You just… move with it.

And that's when you begin to sense it:

This place has a rhythm.

Not a schedule, that's something else entirely. Schedules are imposed, structured, often rigid. Rhythm is looser than that. It's something you fall into rather than follow. Something that exists whether you pay attention to it or not.

In the beginning, you were out of sync with it.

You woke too early or too late. Ate at the wrong times. Misread the pace of conversations, the spacing of silence, the way people occupied time. You were always slightly ahead or slightly behind, like a song playing just off-beat.

Now, you're closer.

Not perfectly aligned, but close enough that the dissonance fades. You move through the day without constantly adjusting. You anticipate things without realizing you're doing it. You've absorbed the timing of the place in ways that feel almost subconscious.

And yet, there's something strange about it.

Because this rhythm, it's not yours.

It works. It carries you. It gives your days a shape that feels natural enough. But every so often, you become aware of it again, like noticing your own breathing after forgetting it was there. And in that moment, there's a slight disconnect.

A question, quiet but persistent:

Is this how I would live if I had chosen it consciously?

Or is this just what happens when you stay somewhere long enough?

The difference is subtle, but it matters.

Because routine has a way of disguising itself as intention.

You wake up at a certain time, not because you've decided it's the best time for you, but because it's when everything around you begins. You eat when others eat. You rest when the city slows down. You adopt patterns not through decision, but through repetition.

And repetition, over time, starts to feel like identity.

This is just how I am now.

But is it?

That's where the rhythm of elsewhere becomes complicated.

It's easy to mistake adaptation for alignment. To assume that because something feels normal, it must also feel right. But normal is just familiarity over time. It doesn't necessarily mean anything deeper than that.

And so you start to notice the gaps.

Small ones at first.

Moments where the day unfolds exactly as expected, and yet feels slightly off. Not wrong, just… not entirely yours. Like wearing clothes that fit well enough but were never tailored for you.

You move through your routines smoothly, efficiently. You know what to do, where to go, how to exist within the structure of this place. But every now and then, there's a pause, a brief interruption in the flow, where you become aware of yourself again.

Not the outsider you were in the first year.

Something else.

Someone who belongs functionally, but not entirely.

And time begins to behave differently here.

In the beginning, it was marked by milestones. First experiences. First mistakes. First moments of understanding. Time moved in noticeable increments because everything was new enough to define it.

Now, it stretches.

Days feel shorter in the moment, but longer in retrospect. Weeks pass without clear distinction. There are fewer markers, fewer moments that stand out as definitively different from the rest. Life becomes continuous in a way that's both calming and disorienting.

You stop asking, What happened today?

Because the answer is usually: the same as yesterday, with slight variations.

And that's not necessarily a bad thing.

There's a quiet stability in it. A sense that life doesn't need to be constantly defined by change or intensity. That it can exist in this more even, sustained way without losing meaning.

But there's also a risk.

Because when everything blends together, it becomes harder to tell whether you're moving forward or simply moving.

The rhythm carries you, but it doesn't tell you where you're going.

And that's the paradox of this stage.

You've achieved what once seemed difficult, normalcy in a place that was never yours. You've adapted, adjusted, integrated. You've found a way to exist here without friction.

But in doing so, you've also stepped into something more ambiguous.

A life that works.

A routine that functions.

A rhythm that holds.

And underneath it all, a quiet, lingering awareness:

You are no longer trying to belong here.

But you're not entirely sure what belonging is supposed to feel like anymore.

Part II

THE UNRAVELING OF EXPECTATIONS

Chapter 4: The Quiet Drift

There's no moment where things fall apart.

That would be easier to understand.

Instead, it happens in a way that's almost impossible to pinpoint, like watching something slowly lose focus. Not enough to blur completely, just enough that the edges soften. The clarity you once had doesn't disappear. It just becomes less precise, less urgent.

You wake up one day and realize you're no longer moving toward anything in particular.

Not because you decided to stop.

But because you never really decided where you were going in the first place.

In the beginning, direction was built in. The act of being somewhere new gave everything a kind of automatic purpose. You were figuring things out, adjusting, progressing, even if that progress was undefined. Movement itself was enough.

Now, movement continues.

But direction fades.

The days begin to take on a uniform shape. Not identical, but close enough that they start to blend. You wake up, go through the motions, interact, return, repeat. Each day contains its own small variations, but they no longer feel distinct. They don't accumulate into anything that resembles momentum.

It's like walking on a treadmill.

There's effort. There's activity. There's even a sense of routine.

But you're not actually going anywhere.

And the strange part is, you don't immediately resist it.

Because nothing feels wrong.

There's no crisis, no obvious dissatisfaction. Life is still functional. In many ways, it's easier than before. You know how to exist here. You've removed most of the friction that once demanded your attention.

But without that friction, something else disappears too.

Friction gave shape to your days.

It created resistance, and resistance made movement feel meaningful. Without it, everything becomes smoother, but also flatter. Less defined.

And so, the drift begins.

Quietly.

You stop setting markers for yourself. Not consciously, you just stop needing them. The urgency that once pushed you forward fades into something softer, less demanding. You tell yourself you'll figure things out eventually. That there's time.

There's always time.

Until time itself becomes part of the blur.

Weeks pass without distinction. You try to recall what you did, what mattered, what stood out, but nothing rises above the surface. It's not that nothing happened. It's that nothing anchored itself strongly enough to be remembered.

The days don't feel long.

They feel interchangeable.

And somewhere in that repetition, a subtle realization begins to take hold:

You're no longer choosing your life day by day.

You're defaulting into it.

That's the part that's hardest to see while it's happening.

Because drifting doesn't feel like losing control.

It feels like letting go of the need to control.

Which, at first, can even seem healthy. Relaxed. Open. Unburdened by constant decision-making. You stop overthinking. You stop forcing direction where none naturally exists.

You just… exist.

But over time, that absence of direction starts to reveal itself in quieter ways.

You hesitate when thinking about the future, not out of fear, but because there's nothing clear to say. Plans feel vague. Goals feel distant, abstract. You tell yourself you're "keeping things open," but beneath that is something less intentional.

You're avoiding definition.

Because definition would require choosing.

And choosing would mean acknowledging that you've been drifting.

So instead, you stay in motion.

Day after day, carried forward by routine, by environment, by the inertia of a life that functions well enough not to demand change.

And that's what makes the drift so effective.

It doesn't disrupt your life.

It replaces its direction.

Chapter 5: The Myth of Simplicity

At some point, you realize the promise was misunderstood.

Not falsely advertised, just misinterpreted.

The idea was simple: leave behind the complexity of your old life, and things would become clearer. Cleaner. Less burdened. A different environment would strip away the noise and reveal something more essential underneath.

And in some ways, it does.

Your life is simpler now.

Fewer obligations. Fewer expectations. Less structure imposed from the outside. You've removed many of the layers that once dictated how you spent your time, who you interacted with, what you were supposed to be working toward.

On the surface, it's exactly what you imagined.

So why does it feel… heavier?

Not externally.

Internally.

That's the part you didn't anticipate.

Because when you remove external complexity, you don't eliminate complexity, you relocate it.

In your previous life, complexity lived outside of you. It was built into systems, expectations, responsibilities. You could point to it, blame it, push against it. It gave you something to react to.

Now, there's less to react against.

And without that external pressure, something else takes its place.

Your own thoughts.

Your own patterns.

Your own unresolved questions.

They move forward to fill the space.

And they're not simpler.

If anything, they're harder to navigate.

Because there's no structure around them.

No clear metrics. No deadlines. No obvious right or wrong direction. Just an open field of possibility that sounds freeing in theory, but in practice feels undefined, even disorienting.

You thought you were escaping complication.

Instead, you've been left alone with it.

That's when the internal noise becomes louder. Not all at once. Not in a way that feels overwhelming. But steadily, persistently.

Questions that used to sit quietly in the background begin to surface more often.

What am I doing here?

Not just geographically, but in a larger sense.

What is this leading to?

What do I actually want?

These aren't new questions.

But without external structure, they're harder to avoid.

Before, your life provided ready-made answers, or at least temporary placeholders. You were working toward something, even if you weren't fully invested in it. You had roles, expectations, trajectories that gave your time a sense of direction.

Now, those placeholders are gone.

And in their absence, you're left with something more honest, but also more demanding.

Choice.

Real choice.

Not the illusion of it, where your options are constrained by circumstance. But the kind that comes with open-ended freedom. The kind that requires you to define your own direction without relying on external systems to do it for you.

And that's where the myth breaks down.

Because simplicity isn't the same as clarity.

You can remove layers from your life and still feel uncertain. You can reduce obligations and still feel overwhelmed.

You can create space, and then realize you don't know what to fill it with.

That's the paradox.

The life you thought would feel lighter begins to feel more complex, not because of what's happening around you, but because of what's happening within you.

Your identity, once supported by structure, now feels less fixed. Your choices, once guided by expectation, now feel more consequential. There's no default path to follow, no clear progression to rely on.

Everything becomes more open.

And openness, it turns out, is not the same as ease.

It's just less defined.

So, the simplicity you were looking for never really existed.

It was always a projection, an assumption that changing your environment would reduce the complexity of being yourself.

But yourself comes with you.

Unchanged at first.

Then slowly, inevitably, more visible.

And once that visibility sets in, you can't unsee it.

The external world may have become simpler.

But internally, things are just beginning to unfold.

Chapter 6: Living Without Edges

At first, it feels like freedom.

Not the dramatic, cinematic kind, the kind people talk about in big, sweeping terms, but something quieter. Subtle. A loosening. The sense that nothing is pressing in on you, nothing is forcing your hand.

Your days are yours.

Not entirely, of course, there are still obligations, still routines, but compared to before, the boundaries are softer. Less defined. You're not being pulled as tightly in any one direction. There's space around your decisions, space around your time.

And space, at the beginning, feels like relief.

Because edges, deadlines, expectations, structures, they create pressure. They demand clarity, even when you don't have it. They force decisions before you're ready to make them. They give your life a shape, but they also confine it.

Now, many of those edges are gone. And what replaces them is something that feels, at least initially, like possibility.

You can wake up later. Or earlier. You can change your plans without consequence. You can decide, mid-day, to go somewhere else, do something else, be someone slightly different than you were yesterday. The rigidity of your previous life has been replaced by something more fluid.

More open.

More yours.

But over time, something begins to shift.

Because edges don't just restrict, they define.

They create contrast. They give your actions weight by placing them within limits. A deadline makes time meaningful. An expectation makes a decision feel deliberate. A boundary gives shape to everything inside it.

Without edges, everything expands.

And when everything expands, it also becomes harder to grasp.

You start to notice it in small ways.

Tasks stretch longer than they need to. Not because they're difficult, but because there's no urgency attached to them. Plans become tentative, easily changed, easily abandoned. You tell yourself you'll do something later, and "later" quietly becomes "not at all."

It's not laziness.

It's diffusion.

Without constraints, your time doesn't break into clear segments. It flows. Which sounds ideal, until you realize that flow without direction is just drift in a different form.

And so the days begin to feel less structured, but also less distinct.

Morning doesn't feel sharply different from afternoon. Weekdays don't feel meaningfully different from weekends. There's a kind of temporal flattening that sets in, where everything exists on the same plane.

You're free to do anything.

Which slowly starts to feel like doing nothing in particular.

That's the paradox no one really prepares you for.

Freedom without constraints doesn't automatically lead to a more intentional life.

Sometimes, it leads to a less defined one.

Because when nothing is required, everything becomes optional.

And when everything is optional, decision-making becomes heavier, not lighter. Every choice carries more weight because it's entirely yours. There's no system to absorb the responsibility, no external structure to guide you.

So you hesitate.

Not dramatically, just enough that decisions blur at the edges. You keep your options open. You avoid committing too strongly to any one path, because committing would mean closing off others.

And in trying to keep everything open, you end up holding everything loosely.

That looseness begins to shape your life.

You move through your days without resistance, but also without tension. And tension, it turns out, is what gives things meaning. It's what makes effort feel purposeful. It's what defines the difference between choosing something and simply allowing it to happen.

Without it, your life becomes easier to live, but harder to interpret.

You start to wonder whether you're actively building something, or just occupying time.

Whether the freedom you have is something you're using, or something that's quietly using you.

Because freedom, when it's not directed, doesn't just sit there waiting.

It disperses.

It spreads itself thin across your days, your decisions, your attention, until everything feels possible but nothing feels necessary.

And necessity, for all its constraints, has a way of clarifying things.

Without it, clarity has to come from you.

And that's the part that's hardest to sustain.

Living without edges means there's nothing to push against.

No resistance to define your movement.

No boundaries to measure yourself within.

Just openness.

Wide, unstructured, and deceptively neutral.

Until you realize that edges weren't just holding you in.

They were also holding you together.

PART III:

RELATIONSHIPS WITHOUT ANCHORS

Chapter 7: Distance Changes Everything

Distance doesn't break things.

It reshapes them.

That's the part people misunderstand. They think of distance as a test, something relationships either survive or fail. As if there's a clear outcome waiting at the end: stronger or weaker, intact or broken.

But distance isn't that decisive.

It's quieter than that. More subtle. It doesn't snap connections, it stretches them. And in that stretching, everything changes shape.

At first, you try to maintain continuity.

You call. You message. You recreate the rhythm of being present, just through different means. Conversations become more intentional, more scheduled. There's an effort to preserve what existed before, to prove that nothing essential has changed.

And for a while, it works.

Or at least, it feels like it does.

Because the connection is still there. Familiar. Recognizable. You can still step into it and feel like the same version of yourself that existed before you left. The same dynamic. The same emotional shorthand.

But over time, something begins to shift.

Not dramatically.

Just enough to notice.

The conversations start to feel slightly delayed, not just in timing, but in relevance. You're no longer sharing the same immediate context. The small details that once connected you, shared environments, mutual experiences, overlapping routines, begin to disappear.

You start explaining more.

And understanding less.

Because explanation fills in facts, but it doesn't recreate presence.

You can describe your day, but the other person isn't in it. They don't feel the pacing, the atmosphere, the subtle interactions that give those details meaning. And the same is true in reverse. Their life continues, just as fully, just as vividly, but at a distance that reduces it to summaries.

And summaries, no matter how detailed, are always incomplete.

That's where the gap begins.

Not an absence of communication, but an absence of shared experience.

You're still connected.

But you're no longer in each other's lives in the same way.

And that distinction matters more than you expect.

Because relationships aren't built only on what is said, they're built on what is lived together. The unspoken moments. The overlap. The casual presence that doesn't require explanation.

Distance removes that layer.

And what's left is something more deliberate, but also more fragile.

You begin to notice it in small ways.

Pauses in conversation that feel slightly longer than they should. Moments where you realize you don't quite know what the other person is thinking, not because they're hiding anything, but because you're no longer aligned in the same rhythm.

You're living parallel lives.

Still connected, but no longer synchronized.

And over time, that lack of synchronization creates a kind of emotional lag. Reactions don't always match. Priorities shift independently. What feels immediate to one person feels distant to the other.

No one is doing anything wrong.

But something is slowly drifting.

The hardest part is that it doesn't feel like loss.

It feels like adjustment.

You adapt. You accept that this is what the relationship looks like now. You lower certain expectations without fully acknowledging that you're doing it. You become more self-contained, less reliant on the connection for daily grounding.

And in doing so, you create space.

Not intentionally.

But inevitably.

That space gets filled, with new routines, new people, new versions of yourself that the other person doesn't fully see.

And that's where distance does its quietest work.

It doesn't remove the relationship.

It changes its center of gravity.

From shared presence…

to managed connection.

And once that shift happens, everything else begins to follow.

Chapter 8: Infidelity Abroad

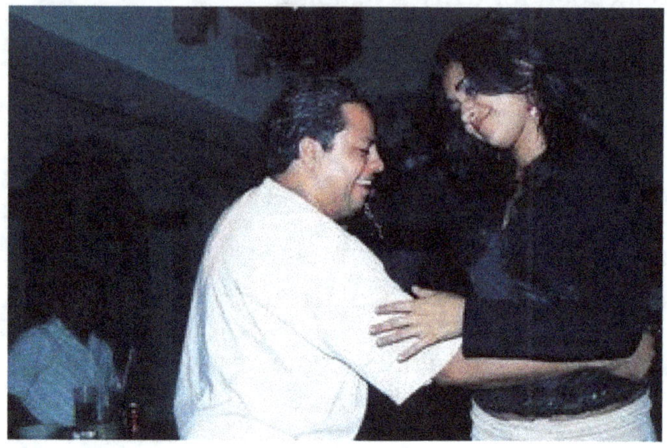

It doesn't start as a decision.

That would be too clear.

Instead, it begins as a shift in context.

A subtle loosening of boundaries that once felt fixed, not because you consciously chose to change them, but because the environment around you no longer reinforces them in the same way.

At home, your life had structure.

Not just in terms of routine, but in terms of identity. You were known in a certain way. Seen consistently by the same people, within the same frameworks. Your actions existed within a network of expectations, social, relational, even moral, that gave them weight.

Here, that network is thinner.

Not gone, but diffused.

You're less observed. Less defined. Less anchored to a single version of yourself. The people around you know you in fragments, in moments, without the full context of who you've been or what you're supposed to be.

And in that fragmentation, something opens up.

Possibility.

Not in a grand, transformative sense, but in small, incremental ways. The ability to behave slightly differently. To test variations of yourself without the same level of consequence. To step outside patterns that once felt fixed.

At first, it's harmless.

A shift in tone. A different kind of conversation. A willingness to engage in ways you might not have before. You tell yourself it's just part of being here, part of adapting, exploring, expanding your experience.

And maybe it is.

But context doesn't just influence behavior.

It redefines it.

Because actions don't exist in isolation, they exist within the frameworks that give them meaning. And when those frameworks change, the meaning shifts with them.

What would have felt like a clear boundary before now feels… less defined.

Not invisible.

Just negotiable.

That's where the rationalization begins.

Quietly.

You don't think of it as crossing a line, because the line itself feels less solid. You tell yourself that things are different here. That the rules are different, not explicitly, but in practice. That distance has already changed the nature of your existing relationships, softened them, stretched them into something less immediate.

You're not replacing anything.

You're just responding to what's in front of you.

That's the logic.

And it works, at least enough to move forward.

Because nothing about it feels dramatic.

There's no moment where you declare a break from your values. No clear decision that marks a before and after. Just a series of small steps, each one easier than the last. A gradual shift from what you would have done to what you're now willing to do.

And the environment supports it.

Not actively, but passively.

You're surrounded by people in similar situations. Other expatriates, other transients, all navigating their own versions of distance, disconnection, and reinvention. Stories circulate, not always openly, but enough that they form a kind of unspoken understanding.

Things happen here.

Not because people are fundamentally different.

But because context makes certain choices feel less absolute.

That's the unsettling part.

Not that behavior changes, but how easily it does.

How quickly something that once felt clear becomes ambiguous. How naturally you adjust your internal narrative to accommodate it. How the version of yourself you thought was fixed turns out to be more flexible than you expected.

And afterwards, there's no single emotion that defines it.

Not guilt in the dramatic sense.

Not even regret, at least not immediately.

Just a quiet awareness.

That something has shifted.

Not just in what you've done, but in how you understand yourself.

Because once you realize that your behavior can change with your environment, it raises a question that's harder to answer than anything that came before:

Were your boundaries ever as fixed as you thought?

Or were they always dependent on where you happened to be standing?

Chapter 9: The Illusion of Reinvention

At some point, the idea becomes tempting.

Not loudly. Not as a declaration. Just a quiet realization that settles in:

No one here really knows you.

Not completely.

They know the version of you that exists now, the one you've presented, the one shaped by your current environment, your current habits, your current choices. But they don't know the full history. The context. The contradictions.

And in that absence, something opens up.

A kind of freedom.

The freedom to adjust.

To emphasize certain traits, minimize others. To lean into parts of yourself that may have been secondary before. To experiment with how you come across, how you behave, how you define yourself in relation to others.

At first, it doesn't feel like reinvention.

It feels like refinement.

You're just becoming a better version of yourself. More relaxed. More open. Less constrained by the expectations that once defined you. You're adapting to a new environment, and in doing so, you're discovering new aspects of who you are.

And some of it is real.

Change does happen. Exposure to new environments, new people, new ways of living, it all shapes you. It would be strange if it didn't.

But alongside that genuine change, something else develops.

Performance.

Subtle at first.

You notice how certain versions of yourself are received. Which traits get attention, approval, interest. Which parts of your personality seem to fit more naturally into this environment. And without consciously deciding to, you begin to lean into those parts.

You become slightly more of what works.

And slightly less of what doesn't.

Not in a dishonest way, at least not intentionally. It's more like editing. Adjusting the emphasis. Presenting a version of yourself that feels aligned with the context you're in.

But over time, the distinction between adaptation and performance starts to blur.

Because when there's no consistent audience, no group of people who've known you across time, you lose a certain kind of accountability to your own continuity. There's no one to say, that's not like you, because no one here knows what you were like before.

So you become whatever feels most natural in the moment.

And "natural" starts to shift depending on where you are, who you're with, what version of yourself fits best in that space.

That's when the question begins to surface:

Is this who I am now?

Or just who I'm being here?

The difference is difficult to pin down.

Because identity has always been, to some extent, situational. You're never exactly the same person in every context. You adjust, adapt, respond. That's normal.

But here, the variation feels wider.

Less anchored.

There's no central version pulling everything back into alignment. No fixed point that all these variations connect to. Just a series of overlapping identities, each one shaped by circumstance.

And without realizing it, you begin to rely on that flexibility.

It becomes easier to step into different versions of yourself than to define a single, consistent one. Easier to perform than to commit. Easier to adapt than to decide.

That's the illusion.

That you're becoming someone new.

When in reality, you may just be becoming less defined.

Because reinvention suggests direction.

A movement from one clear state to another.

But what's happening here isn't linear.

It's fragmented.

Pieces of identity shifting, rearranging, responding to context without necessarily forming something cohesive. You're not replacing your old self with a new one, you're layering variations on top of each other, without fully resolving them.

And eventually, that creates a kind of quiet instability.

Not visible from the outside.

But noticeable from within.

You start to feel slightly disconnected from your own continuity. Like the person you were before is still there, but less accessible. Like the person you are now depends too much on where you are and who you're with.

And somewhere in that awareness, the illusion begins to fade.

Because becoming someone new should feel like clarity.

This feels more like diffusion.

Chapter 10: Intimacy Without Permanence

The connections happen quickly.

Faster than you expect.

There's a kind of acceleration to relationships in this environment, a compression of time that makes things move at a different pace. Conversations go deeper, sooner. Boundaries soften more quickly. There's less hesitation, less gradual buildup.

It feels immediate.

Intense.

Real.

And in many ways, it is.

Because there's an understanding, sometimes spoken, often not, that time is limited. That people come and go. That whatever exists now may not exist later. And that awareness creates a kind of urgency.

You don't hold back in the same way.

You skip steps.

You move past the slow process of getting to know someone and into something that feels more direct, more emotionally charged. There's less concern about long-term consequences, less emphasis on gradual development.

You connect where you are.

Fully, if only for a while.

And those connections can feel surprisingly strong.

Stronger, sometimes, than relationships that took much longer to form. There's an honesty in them, a willingness to be open, to share, to engage without the usual layers of hesitation.

But that intensity comes with a trade-off.

Permanence.

Or rather, the lack of it.

Because while the emotional connection may form quickly, it doesn't have the same foundation. It isn't built on shared history, on long-term continuity, on the slow accumulation of experience that gives relationships depth over time.

It's built on immediacy.

On the present moment.

And the present, by definition, doesn't last.

That's where the pattern begins to emerge.

Connections form.

They deepen.

They feel meaningful, sometimes unexpectedly so.

And then, just as naturally, they dissolve.

Not always dramatically. Not always with conflict or clear endings. Sometimes they just fade, as circumstances shift. Someone leaves. Priorities change. The environment that brought you together no longer exists in the same way.

And without that shared context, the connection struggles to hold.

Because it was never designed to.

That's the part that's hardest to accept.

That something can feel real, significant, even important, and still not be built to last.

You start to recognize the cycle.

The way intensity substitutes for longevity. The way emotional closeness can develop quickly, but without the structure needed to sustain it. The way goodbyes become less surprising, even when they still carry weight.

And over time, your relationship to intimacy begins to change.

You become more open, in some ways. More willing to engage, to connect, to experience something fully in the moment without overthinking where it's going.

But at the same time, you become more guarded in others.

Not outwardly.

Internally.

Because you start to anticipate the ending.

Even in the beginning.

There's a part of you that holds back, not from the connection itself, but from the idea of permanence. You stop assuming that things will continue. You stop building expectations around the future.

You stay present.

But you also stay aware.

And that awareness creates a subtle distance.

Even in moments of closeness.

That's the paradox.

You can feel deeply connected to someone…

and still know, at the same time, that the connection is temporary.

And eventually, that dual awareness begins to shape how you experience everything.

Not just relationships, but time, attachment, even yourself.

Because when nothing feels permanent, everything becomes more immediate.

More intense.

But also more fleeting.

And somewhere in that cycle, intimacy stops being about building something lasting.

And starts becoming something else entirely:

An experience to be felt…

before it disappears.

PART IV:

THE EXPAT MICROCOSM

Chapter 11: A World of Transients

At first, it feels like a community.

You meet people quickly, easily. There's a kind of openness that makes introductions feel less formal, less guarded. Conversations start without much effort. Plans form without much hesitation. You're surrounded by others who are, in some version of the same situation: not from here, not fully rooted, existing in a space that feels temporary, even when no one says it out loud.

And that shared condition creates an immediate connection.

You don't have to explain certain things.

The dislocation. The adjustment. The quiet awareness that this isn't permanent, even if you don't know what comes next. It's understood, almost instinctively. Everyone carries some version of it.

And that becomes the social glue.

Not deep compatibility, necessarily, but shared displacement.

You gather in the same places. Bars, cafés, apartments that feel slightly improvised. Conversations overlap. Names circulate.

There's a sense of being part of something, even if that something is loosely defined.

It feels like belonging.

Or at least, something close enough to it.

But over time, the nature of that community starts to reveal itself.

Because people don't stay.

Not all at once, not dramatically, but steadily. Someone leaves. Another plans to. Someone new arrives, filling the same space, asking the same questions you once asked, moving through the same early stages you've already passed.

The group shifts, constantly.

Familiar faces disappear. New ones take their place. The overall shape remains, but the individuals within it change. And after a while, you begin to notice the pattern.

This isn't a stable community.

It's a rotating one.

Held together not by permanence, but by overlap.

People are there at the same time, for a while. Long enough to form connections, to create shared experiences, to feel like something real is happening. But beneath that, there's an unspoken understanding:

This is temporary.

Even if no one knows exactly when it will end.

That temporariness affects everything.

Relationships form faster because there's less time. Social circles become more fluid because nothing is fixed. You meet people in concentrated bursts, building familiarity quickly, skipping the slow, gradual process that usually defines connection.

It's efficient.

And in some ways, exciting.

There's always movement. Always new energy. Always the sense that something is happening, that life is active, dynamic, in motion.

But there's also a limit to how deep it goes.

Because depth requires continuity.

And continuity is the one thing this environment doesn't provide.

You start to notice that conversations rarely build on each other over long periods. That relationships, while intense, don't always evolve. That the community itself doesn't accumulate history in the way more permanent ones do.

It resets.

Again and again.

New people arrive, bringing the same curiosity, the same early excitement, the same questions you once had. And you find yourself repeating explanations, retelling stories, reintroducing parts of yourself that no longer feel new, but are new to them.

You become, in a way, both participant and observer.

Part of the cycle, but also aware of it.

And that awareness creates a subtle distance.

Because once you see the pattern, it's hard to fully lose yourself in it.

You know that the connections you're forming exist within a limited timeframe. That the sense of community, while real, is also conditional. Dependent on proximity, on timing, on the temporary alignment of people who are all, in some sense, passing through.

A world of transients.

Connected, but not anchored.

Shared, but not stable.

And somewhere within it, you begin to wonder:

Is this a community…

or just a series of overlapping exits?

Chapter 12: Conversations on Repeat

After a while, you start to notice the script.

Not immediately.

At first, every conversation feels new, different people, different backgrounds, different paths that led them here. There's variety in the details, enough to make each interaction feel distinct.

But over time, the structure underneath those conversations begins to repeat.

It starts the same way.

Where are you from?

How long have you been here?

What brought you?

The answers vary, but only within a certain range. Work. Escape. Curiosity. Opportunity. A vague sense of wanting something different. The specifics change, but the themes stay the same.

And you begin to recognize them.

Not just in others, but in yourself.

You hear your own responses becoming more polished, more automatic. Stories you've told enough times that they no longer require thought. Explanations that once felt personal now delivered with a kind of practiced ease.

You're not being dishonest.

But you're not entirely present, either.

Because you already know how the conversation goes.

After the basics, it moves into shared observations. The quirks of the place. The differences from home. The things that surprised you, frustrated you, amused you. There's a rhythm to it, a predictable progression that feels comfortable precisely because it's familiar.

And for a while, that familiarity is enough.

It creates connection.

Or at least, the appearance of it.

But gradually, something begins to feel off.

Not wrong, just repetitive.

You realize that while the conversations are engaging in the moment, they don't always lead anywhere. They don't build. They don't deepen over time. Each one exists largely on its own, disconnected from the next.

There's no accumulation.

No sense that you're developing a shared narrative with the people around you. Instead, you're having variations of the same exchange, over and over, with different participants.

It's like listening to different versions of the same song.

The melody shifts slightly. The details change. But the structure remains.

Predictable.

Contained.

And eventually, that predictability becomes noticeable enough that you can't ignore it.

You start to anticipate responses before they're given. You recognize the patterns in how people present themselves, how they frame their experiences, how they position their reasons for being here.

And in doing so, the conversations lose some of their immediacy.

They become less about discovery…

and more about confirmation.

That everyone is, in some way, telling a version of the same story.

Including you.

That's when the lack of continuity becomes more apparent.

Because conversations, like relationships, need time to develop layers. To move beyond the surface, beyond the rehearsed narratives, into something more specific, more nuanced, more real.

But in a world of transients, time is limited.

So most interactions stay within a certain range, deep enough to feel meaningful, but not extended enough to become fully rooted.

You touch on ideas.

You share perspectives.

But rarely do you return to them in a way that builds something lasting.

And over time, that creates a subtle sense of detachment.

Not from the people themselves, but from the process.

You begin to feel like you're participating in a loop.

Engaging, responding, connecting, but within a framework that resets too often to sustain anything beyond the immediate moment.

And that's the quiet shift.

When conversation stops being a pathway to deeper understanding…

and starts becoming a pattern you move through.

Comfortable.

Familiar.

And just repetitive enough to make you wonder what's missing.

Chapter 13: Watching Others Become Someone Else

It's easier to see in other people.

That's how it starts.

You notice small changes at first, subtle shifts in behavior, tone, the way someone carries themselves. Nothing dramatic enough to call out. Just enough to register. Someone who used to be reserved becomes more outgoing. Someone structured becomes looser, more improvisational. Someone who seemed grounded starts to drift in ways that are harder to define.

At first, you interpret it as adaptation.

Of course people change here. That's the point. New environment, new influences, new freedoms. It would be strange if everyone stayed exactly the same.

But over time, the changes become more noticeable.

More distinct.

It's not just that people are adjusting, it's that they're becoming different versions of themselves. Not entirely new, but altered in ways that don't always seem connected to who they were before.

And the longer you stay, the more examples you accumulate.

You see the patterns.

The person who arrives cautious, observant, slightly overwhelmed, and within months becomes fully integrated into the social rhythm, moving easily through spaces that once felt unfamiliar. The person who came with clear intentions, clear boundaries, and gradually lets those edges soften, then blur.

The person who said they'd only stay a year.

And is still here.

But not quite the same.

At first, these shifts are interesting.

Almost fascinating.

You watch people evolve in real time, without the slow pacing that usually defines change. There's a compression to it, like identity is being reshaped faster than it would be anywhere else. Fewer constraints, fewer consistent reference points, so the process accelerates.

But then, something else begins to surface.

A question.

Not about them.

About you.

Because the more you observe these changes, the harder it becomes to maintain the assumption that you're somehow separate from them. That you're simply watching, unaffected, maintaining a consistent sense of self while others adapt.

That assumption starts to feel less stable.

You begin to recognize familiar patterns in their shifts, patterns that echo your own experiences. The way they justify certain choices. The way they describe their transformation. The way they reconcile who they were with who they're becoming.

It all starts to sound… familiar.

Too familiar to ignore.

And that's when the observation turns inward.

You start to ask the same questions, but directed at yourself.

What has changed?

Not on the surface, that's easy to see. Your routines, your environment, your social circles. Those are obvious.

But underneath that.

The way you think. The way you respond. The way you define yourself in relation to everything around you.

How much of that is different?

And more importantly, when did it change?

Because unlike the first year, where every shift felt visible, noticeable, almost documented in real time, these changes are quieter. They don't announce themselves. They accumulate gradually, below the level of immediate awareness.

You don't feel like a different person.

But when you look closely, the continuity isn't as solid as it once seemed.

That's the unsettling part.

Not that change is happening, but that it's happening without clear markers. Without a defined beginning or end. Without a moment where you can say, this is where I became someone else.

Instead, it's spread out.

Across conversations, decisions, environments. Across the subtle adjustments you've made to fit, to adapt, to exist more easily within this context.

And once you see it in others, you can't fully avoid seeing it in yourself.

You start to notice the ways you've shifted your boundaries. The way your reactions have changed. The way certain things that once felt unfamiliar now feel normal.

Expected, even.

And that realization creates a strange kind of distance.

Not from others, but from your own sense of stability.

Because if identity can shift this easily, this quietly, then what anchors it?

What makes it consistent?

Is there a core that remains unchanged, or is that just another assumption, one that holds until the environment changes enough to challenge it?

Watching others become someone else forces you to confront a possibility that's harder to ignore than anything that came before:

That identity isn't as fixed as you thought.

That it's shaped, continuously, by context, by environment, by the subtle pressures and freedoms of where you are.

And that you are not outside of that process.

You're in it.

Just like everyone else.

The only difference is how long it takes you to notice.

PART V:

MORAL DRIFT

Chapter 14: Different Rules Apply Here

No one says it out loud.

There's no meeting, no agreement, no moment where the rules are formally rewritten. And yet, over time, a quiet understanding begins to take hold:

Things are different here.

Not in obvious ways, laws still exist, social norms still operate, but in the way those rules are felt. The way they're interpreted. The way they're applied to your own behavior.

Back home, your actions existed within a dense network of expectations.

Family, long-term friends, professional environments, cultural familiarity, all of it created a kind of invisible structure around you. Not just telling you what was acceptable, but reinforcing it constantly. Your behavior had context. Continuity. Consequences that extended beyond the immediate moment.

Here, that structure is thinner.

Not absent, but reduced.

You're less embedded. Less accountable in ways that feel immediate. The people around you don't share your full history. They don't know the version of you that existed before this. And more importantly, they're not necessarily connected to the life you'll return to, if you return at all.

That separation creates a kind of psychological distance.

And distance changes how rules feel.

What once seemed fixed now feels more flexible. Not irrelevant, just adjustable. Dependent on context. Influenced by circumstance.

You start to notice it in small justifications.

This is different.

This doesn't really count the same way.

No one here sees it the way it would be seen back home.

And those thoughts don't feel like excuses.

They feel reasonable.

Because in some ways, they are.

Cultural context does shift behavior. What's acceptable in one place may not be in another. Social norms aren't universal, they're localized, fluid, shaped by environment. Adapting to that isn't inherently wrong. It's part of existing within a different system.

But adaptation has a boundary.

And here, that boundary becomes harder to define.

Because you're not just navigating a new culture.

You're navigating your own relationship to it.

Deciding, often unconsciously, which rules are external, belonging to the place you came from, and which ones are internal, something you carry regardless of where you are.

And that distinction isn't always clear.

Some things feel obviously constant. Core principles, fundamental beliefs. You assume those won't change. That they exist outside of environment, outside of context.

But others?

They start to shift.

Gradually.

You become more permissive with yourself. More willing to interpret situations in ways that align with what you want, rather than what you once believed was right. You don't abandon your values, you adjust them. Subtly, carefully, often without fully acknowledging that you're doing it.

And the environment supports this.

Not by encouraging it directly, but by not resisting it.

You're surrounded by people making similar adjustments. Living in similar ambiguity. Navigating the same blurred lines between who they were and who they are here. There's no strong corrective force pulling you back to your original framework.

So the framework evolves.

Quietly.

What once felt like a clear boundary becomes a gray area. What once required justification becomes easier to accept. What once would have stood out now blends into the background of a place where everyone is, in some way, operating under slightly different rules.

And eventually, you stop questioning it as much.

Not because you've resolved the tension.

But because the tension itself becomes normalized.

That's the shift.

When "this is different" stops being an observation…

and starts becoming a justification.

Chapter 15: The Slippery Slope

No one changes all at once.

That's the comforting assumption.

That if something significant were happening, if you were really crossing a line, really becoming someone different, you would notice it. There would be a moment. A clear break. A before and after you could point to and say, that's where it happened.

But it doesn't work like that.

It never does.

Change, especially this kind of change, is incremental.

So small at each step that it feels almost insignificant. Easy to overlook. Easy to explain. Easy to justify as an exception rather than a shift.

You don't move from one version of yourself to another.

You move slightly.

Then slightly again.

And again.

Each step feels manageable. Reasonable. Within a range you can still recognize as "you." There's no single decision that feels like a departure, just a series of adjustments that, taken individually, don't seem to mean much.

That's what makes it effective.

Because if each step feels acceptable, the direction they're taking you in doesn't immediately register.

You adapt to each new position as it becomes your baseline.

What felt unfamiliar becomes normal. What felt questionable becomes understandable. What once required justification becomes something you no longer think about at all.

And the distance between where you started and where you are now grows quietly.

Almost invisibly.

You only notice it when you look back.

When something, an old conversation, a memory, a moment of reflection, reminds you of how you used to think, how you used to respond, what you used to consider obvious.

And the contrast is… uncomfortable.

Not because you've done anything dramatically wrong.

But because the shift wasn't conscious.

You didn't decide to change.

You just… did.

That's the unsettling part of the slippery slope.

It doesn't feel like losing control.

It feels like maintaining it, at every step.

You make choices. You weigh options. You justify outcomes. At no point do you feel like you've abandoned your sense of judgment. In fact, each decision feels like a continuation of it.

And yet, the result is different.

Because judgment itself has been adjusting along the way.

Quietly recalibrating.

Each step slightly altering your internal standards, so that the next step feels just as acceptable as the last.

That's how the slope works.

Not as a sudden drop, but as a gradual incline you don't realize you're climbing until the ground behind you is far enough away to notice.

And by then, returning isn't simple.

Not because you can't, but because you're no longer entirely sure where "back" is. The version of yourself you're comparing against feels distant. Less immediate. Almost like a reference point rather than a current reality.

You've adapted to where you are now.

This feels normal.

Even if it wouldn't have before.

And that realization brings a different kind of awareness.

Not dramatic. Not overwhelming.

Just clear.

That change doesn't need a defining moment to be real.

It just needs time.

And a series of steps small enough…

that you never thought to stop walking.

Chapter 16: Justifying Everything

It doesn't feel like lying.

That's the first thing.

If it did, if there were a clear sense of dishonesty, a sharp awareness that you were telling yourself something untrue, it might be easier to stop. Easier to recognize the gap between what you believe and what you're doing.

But it doesn't happen like that.

Instead, it feels like explaining.

Clarifying.

Contextualizing.

You're not denying anything, you're just interpreting it in a way that makes sense. A way that fits. A way that allows your actions to remain aligned with the version of yourself you still believe you are.

That's how the internal narrative forms.

Quietly.

You begin to build explanations, not for others, but for yourself. Stories that connect your choices to reasonable causes. Circumstances. Situations. The environment. The fact that things here are different.

And those explanations aren't entirely false.

That's what makes them effective.

There are differences. Context does matter. Situations are more complex than simple right and wrong. You're not inventing a new reality, you're selecting from the one that exists, emphasizing the parts that support your behavior.

It's not fabrication.

It's framing.

And once you start framing things a certain way, it becomes easier to maintain.

Because consistency matters, not just in what you do, but in how you understand what you do. You need your actions to make sense within your own worldview. You need to believe that you're still operating within your values, even if those values have become more flexible than they once were.

So the narrative adjusts.

Not abruptly.

Gradually.

You redefine intention. You focus on context. You soften the language around certain choices. What might once have been described in clear terms now becomes more nuanced, more conditional.

It's not this.

It's something like this, but under these circumstances, and for these reasons.

And the more detailed the explanation becomes, the more convincing it feels.

Not because it's objectively stronger, but because it allows you to stay consistent with yourself.

That's the real function of justification.

Not to defend your actions to others.

But to preserve your internal coherence.

To avoid the discomfort of contradiction.

Because contradiction creates tension.

And tension demands resolution.

So instead of changing the behavior, you change the interpretation of it.

You adjust the meaning until it fits.

And once it fits, the tension fades.

At least on the surface.

But underneath, something remains.

A faint awareness that the explanation is doing more work than it should. That the narrative is slightly more elaborate than necessary. That you're not just describing your actions, you're managing them.

That awareness doesn't disappear.

It just becomes easier to ignore.

And that's where humor enters.

Not as a defense at first.

Just as a way of talking about things.

You make light of situations. Turn them into stories. Add a layer of irony, a hint of self-awareness that signals you understand the complexity of what you're doing.

You joke about it.

Not harshly. Not critically. Just enough to create distance.

Because humor does something useful.

It diffuses.

It allows you to acknowledge something without fully confronting it. To bring it into the open, but in a way that softens its impact. If something can be laughed at, it feels less serious. Less absolute. Less in need of resolution.

So you laugh.

With others, especially.

Because they understand.

They're operating within similar frameworks, navigating similar ambiguities. The humor becomes shared, a kind of shorthand for the unspoken understanding that things aren't as clear as they seem, and that everyone is, in some way, adjusting their own narrative to make sense of it.

It creates connection.

But it also creates cover.

Because as long as something remains within the realm of humor, it doesn't have to be fully examined. It doesn't have to be resolved. It can exist in that in-between space, acknowledged, but not confronted.

And over time, that becomes a pattern.

You explain.

You justify.

You reframe.

And when the edges of those explanations start to feel thin, you soften them with humor.

Not to deceive.

But to maintain balance.

Because without that balance, you'd have to face something more direct.

That your actions and your values are no longer perfectly aligned.

And that the distance between them isn't accidental.

It's been built.

Step by step.

Explanation by explanation.

Story by story.

Until the narrative itself becomes part of the structure holding everything in place.

And once that structure exists, it's hard to see where the truth ends…and the justification begins.

PART VI:

BETWEEN WORLDS

Chapter 17: Looking Back at Home

Distance doesn't just separate you from a place.

It reshapes it.

The version of home you carry with you isn't static, it evolves, quietly, as your relationship to it changes. At first, it remains familiar, almost intact. You think of it as it was when you left, clear, immediate, emotionally accessible.

But over time, that clarity softens.

Details fade. Not completely, but enough that they begin to reorganize themselves. Certain memories become sharper, more defined, while others recede into the background. What remains isn't a complete picture, it's a curated one.

Selective.

And that selectivity isn't random.

In the beginning, you tend to focus on what you've left behind, the structure, the familiarity, the ease of understanding how things work. There's a kind of nostalgia that forms, even if you didn't feel particularly attached before you left.

You remember the convenience.

The predictability.

The sense that life had a clearer shape.

But as time passes, another layer emerges.

You start to see what you couldn't see before.

The assumptions that felt invisible when you were inside them. The patterns that seemed normal simply because they were familiar. The expectations that shaped your behavior without ever being explicitly questioned.

Distance gives you perspective.

But perspective isn't neutral.

It alters emphasis.

Things that once felt important begin to seem arbitrary. Things that once felt fixed begin to look constructed. You start to notice how much of what you considered "normal" was simply a product of environment.

Not universal.

Just consistent.

And once you see that, it's hard to unsee.

You begin to reinterpret your past life, not as a stable reference point, but as one version among many. One system, with its own rules, its own pressures, its own internal logic.

No more or less real than the one you're living in now.

Just different.

That realization shifts something fundamental.

Because "home" was always more than a place, it was a framework. A set of expectations that gave your life structure, direction, meaning. It defined what progress looked like, what success meant, what choices were considered reasonable or necessary.

From a distance, that framework becomes visible.

And once it's visible, it becomes optional.

That's the part that creates tension.

Because you can no longer fully return to it in the same way.

Even if you go back physically, the perspective you've gained doesn't disappear. You've seen outside the system. You've experienced alternatives. You've recognized that what once felt inevitable is, in fact, conditional.

And that changes how you relate to it.

You start to question things you once accepted without hesitation. Paths that once seemed obvious now feel more like choices. Expectations that once guided you now feel like suggestions, ones you may or may not want to follow.

But at the same time, something else happens.

The version of home you're evaluating isn't entirely accurate.

It's filtered.

Shaped by distance, by memory, by the contrast with your current environment. You're not seeing it as it is, you're seeing it as it appears from where you stand now.

And that perspective is just as constructed as the one you had before.

That's the paradox.

Distance gives clarity.

But it also introduces distortion.

You're seeing more, and less, at the same time.

And somewhere between those two, your understanding of home begins to shift.

From something fixed…

to something relative.

Chapter 18: The Myth of Stability

For a long time, you believed in stability.

Not consciously, maybe, but as a background assumption. The idea that there was a "normal" life. A path that, once followed, would lead to something consistent. Predictable. Structured in a way that made sense over time.

You didn't have to fully commit to it to believe in it.

It was just there.

A reference point.

Something you could return to, even if you chose not to.

That's part of what made leaving feel temporary in the beginning.

The assumption that stability existed elsewhere. That you had stepped away from it, but not lost it. That it was still available, waiting, unchanged.

But over time, that assumption begins to weaken.

Not because your current life feels unstable, though it might, but because you start to question whether stability exists in the way you once imagined.

You begin to see patterns.

Not just in your own experience, but in others. The people around you, expatriates, transients, individuals navigating similar uncertainties, they often describe their lives in terms of transition. Movement. Change.

At first, it's easy to contrast that with the idea of a more "stable" life back home.

But the longer you observe, the less clear that distinction becomes.

Because when you look more closely, really look, you start to notice that the people you once considered stable aren't as fixed as they seemed.

Their lives change too.

Careers shift. Relationships evolve or dissolve. Priorities realign. What looked like a steady trajectory from the outside reveals itself, over time, to be just as fluid as anything else.

The difference isn't in the presence of change.

It's in how it's framed.

Some environments package change within structure. They give it a narrative, progression, advancement, development, that makes it feel stable, even when it isn't. There's a sense of continuity that smooths over the underlying movement.

Other environments expose that movement more directly.

Less structure. Fewer predefined paths. More visible transitions.

But the movement itself?

It's everywhere.

That's when the idea of stability starts to feel less like a reality…

and more like a story.

A way of organizing experience so that it feels manageable. Predictable. Contained.

Not false, exactly.

But incomplete.

Because what you're beginning to see is that instability isn't something you stepped into by leaving.

It's something that was always there.

You've just removed the structures that were masking it.

And that realization shifts the question.

It's no longer about finding stability in a place, a career, a relationship, or a set of choices.

It's about understanding that stability, as you imagined it, may not exist in a fixed form.

That life doesn't settle into a permanent state of clarity.

It moves.

Continuously.

And the sense of stability comes not from eliminating that movement, but from how you relate to it.

That's the uncomfortable part.

Because it removes the idea of a final arrival.

No point where everything locks into place and remains there. No version of life that resolves all uncertainty and replaces it with something permanent.

Just different configurations.

Different balances between structure and freedom, certainty and ambiguity, movement and pause.

And once you see that, you can't return to the old assumption.

That somewhere, somehow, there is a version of life that is fully stable.

Instead, you're left with something less reassuring, but more honest:

That instability isn't the exception.

It's the condition.

Chapter 19: Nowhere Feels Permanent

At some point, the question changes.

It's no longer Where do I belong?

It becomes:

Do I belong anywhere at all?

Not in a dramatic, existential sense. Not something you sit down and consciously wrestle with. It's quieter than that. More subtle. A feeling that surfaces in moments, uninvited, unresolved.

You notice it when you think about going back.

Home.

The place that once felt fixed, familiar, unquestioned. The place that, for a long time, existed in your mind as a kind of anchor. Something stable. Something you could return to and immediately recognize as yours.

But now, when you picture it, something feels… off.

Not wrong.

Just distant.

You can imagine being there. You can recall the routines, the environments, the expectations. But you can't fully place yourself back into them. There's a slight disconnect, like trying to step into a version of your life that no longer fits the same way.

You've changed.

And more importantly, your perspective has.

The things that once felt natural now feel more deliberate. More constructed. You're aware of the framework in a way you weren't before. You can see the assumptions, the patterns, the expectations that shape life there, and that awareness creates distance.

Even before you return.

But then you look at where you are now.

And the same feeling appears.

This place, too, doesn't fully hold you.

You've adapted. You function here. You understand the rhythms, the social structures, the unspoken rules. In many ways, you move through this environment with ease.

But underneath that ease, there's a recognition:

You're still not from here.

Not completely.

There are layers you don't access. Histories you're not part of. A deeper continuity that exists independently of your presence. You can participate, but you don't fully belong to the structure that defines it.

And so you exist in both places.

But not entirely in either.

That's the in-between.

Not a physical location, but a state.

A way of existing where your reference points no longer align cleanly. Where the place you came from feels partially unfamiliar, and the place you are feels partially incomplete.

You're connected to both.

And fully anchored to neither.

At first, this feels like freedom.

The ability to move between worlds. To not be confined to a single identity, a single place, a single framework. You can step in and out, adjust, adapt, exist across boundaries that once felt fixed.

But over time, that freedom reveals its cost.

Because belonging isn't just about access.

It's about continuity.

It's about being part of something that extends beyond your individual presence. A shared history. A stable context. A sense that your place within it isn't temporary or conditional.

And in the in-between, that continuity is harder to find.

Your relationships are more fluid. Your environment more transient. Your identity more adaptable, but also less rooted. You're constantly adjusting, recalibrating, positioning yourself within shifting contexts.

It works.

But it doesn't settle.

That's the difference.

You can build a life here.

You can create routines, connections, even meaning.

But there's a quiet awareness underneath it all:

This could change.

And not in some distant, abstract way, but at any time. Because the structures around you are less fixed. The people, the environment, even your own trajectory, they all exist within a kind of open-ended uncertainty.

And that uncertainty becomes part of your baseline.

You stop expecting permanence.

Not out of pessimism, but out of experience.

You've seen how easily things shift. How quickly contexts change. How identity, relationships, and environment can all be redefined without a single clear moment marking the transition.

So you adjust.

You hold things more lightly. You engage fully, but without the same assumption of continuity. You stop building your sense of self around permanence, because permanence no longer feels reliable.

And in doing so, you become something else.

Not rootless.

But unrooted.

There's a difference.

Rootless suggests absence, nothing to connect to.

Unrooted suggests movement, connections that exist, but don't anchor you in one place.

You carry them with you.

But they don't hold you down.

And that's where the in-between becomes both a space and a condition.

You're not waiting to arrive somewhere.

You're not trying to return to where you started.

You're existing within the gap between the two.

Where nothing feels fully permanent.

And maybe never will again.

PART VII:

RECKONING WITH THE SELF

Chapter 20: The Person You Become

There's no single moment where you recognize it.

No clear line separating who you were from who you are now. If anything, the change feels incomplete, like something still in progress, still shifting, still refusing to settle into a final form.

And yet, when you look closely, the difference is undeniable.

Not in obvious ways.

You still sound like yourself. Think like yourself. React in ways that feel familiar enough not to raise alarm. There's continuity there, just enough to maintain the sense that you're still the same person.

But underneath that continuity, something has shifted.

Subtly.

Permanently.

You notice it in contrast.

When you think about how you used to see things, what felt certain, what felt obvious, what felt unquestioned. The clarity you once had about certain ideas, certain boundaries, certain expectations.

That clarity isn't gone.

But it's less absolute.

More conditional.

You've seen too much variation, too many different ways of living, thinking, choosing, to fully return to a single, fixed perspective. What once felt universal now feels contextual. What once felt stable now feels dependent on circumstance.

And that awareness changes you.

Not dramatically.

But fundamentally.

You become less rigid.

More open, in some ways. More willing to accept ambiguity, to exist without clear answers, to hold conflicting ideas without needing to resolve them immediately.

But that openness comes with a cost.

You're also less certain.

Less anchored to a defined sense of who you are and what you stand for. The edges that once gave your identity structure have softened. The boundaries that once felt fixed now feel negotiable.

You've gained flexibility.

But lost some clarity.

And that trade-off isn't easy to evaluate.

Because it doesn't present itself as purely positive or negative. It's both. At the same time. You're more adaptable, more capable of navigating complexity, but also more aware of how little is truly fixed.

And that awareness follows you.

Into decisions.

Into relationships.

Into the way you think about your own future.

You start to question not just what you want, but how stable that wanting actually is. Whether your preferences are consistent, or shaped by the environment you're in. Whether the person you are now will still feel like "you" in a different context.

And the answer isn't clear.

Because the version of yourself you're comparing against, the one from before, no longer feels fully accessible.

You remember it.

But you don't entirely inhabit it anymore.

That's the quiet realization.

You haven't just experienced change.

You've become it.

Not a new person, exactly.

But a different configuration of the same one.

And that difference isn't temporary.

It doesn't fade when you return to familiar places, or reconnect with old patterns. It stays with you, embedded in how you see, how you interpret, how you move through the world.

Which means there's no going back to who you were.

Only forward…

as someone you're still learning to understand.

Chapter 21: Freedom Revisited

At the beginning, freedom was simple.

Or at least, it seemed that way.

It meant leaving.

Breaking away from structure, expectation, routine. Creating space where there had been constraint. Choosing your own path instead of following one that had already been laid out.

Freedom was movement.

Possibility.

The absence of limitation.

And for a while, that definition held.

It felt accurate. Satisfying. Even necessary. You experienced the immediate benefits, the ability to shape your days, redefine your priorities, exist outside of systems that once felt fixed.

It was everything you thought it would be.

Until it wasn't.

Because over time, the absence of constraint reveals something else:

The presence of responsibility.

Total responsibility.

Not the kind that comes from obligation, but the kind that comes from choice. When nothing is imposed, everything becomes yours to decide. Not just the big things, where you live, what you do, but the small, continuous decisions that make up the structure of your life.

How you spend your time.

What you prioritize.

Who you become.

And without external frameworks to guide those decisions, they become heavier.

Not because they're harder in isolation, but because there's nothing to defer to. No default path. No built-in justification. Every choice reflects back on you more directly, because it isn't shaped by expectation, it's shaped by intention.

Or the lack of it.

That's when freedom begins to feel different.

Less like release.

More like exposure.

You're no longer constrained by structure, but you're also no longer supported by it. The boundaries that once limited you also provided definition. They gave your life a shape, a direction that didn't have to be constantly questioned.

Now, that shape has to come from you.

And that's not always easy to sustain.

Because freedom doesn't come with instructions.

It doesn't tell you what to do with itself.

It simply creates space.

And space, on its own, is neutral.

It can be filled with intention, or drift.

Clarity, or confusion.

Purpose, or repetition.

That's the part that complicates the original idea.

Freedom isn't inherently meaningful.

It becomes meaningful only through what you do with it.

And what you do with it isn't always consistent.

Some days, it feels expansive. Energizing. Like you're actively shaping something that belongs entirely to you.

Other days, it feels uncertain. Directionless. Like the absence of structure has removed not just limitation, but clarity.

Both are true.

That's the paradox.

Freedom is a gift.

Because it allows you to choose.

But it's also a burden.

Because it requires you to choose.

Continuously.

Without guarantees.

Without a clear endpoint.

And without the comfort of knowing that the path you're on is the "right" one in any objective sense.

You're not following a system.

You're creating one.

And creation is inherently unstable.

It involves uncertainty, revision, doubt. It requires you to move forward without complete information, to make decisions without knowing how they'll hold over time.

That's what freedom actually is.

Not the absence of constraint.

But the presence of possibility…

combined with the responsibility to shape it.

And once you understand that, the idea of freedom doesn't disappear.

It deepens.

Becomes more complex.

Less idealized.

But more real.

Because now it's not just something you wanted.

It's something you're living.

Fully.

With all the weight, and all the openness, that comes with it.

Chapter 22: The Weight of Choice

At some point, the realization settles in, not suddenly, but with a quiet persistence that's hard to ignore:

There is no default anymore.

No path you can step onto without thinking. No sequence of decisions that carries you forward simply because it's what people do. The structures that once absorbed choice, career tracks, social expectations, familiar timelines, have loosened or disappeared entirely.

And what's left is open.

Completely open.

At first, this feels like the culmination of everything you wanted.

To not be confined. To not be directed by systems you didn't choose. To exist outside of prewritten narratives about what your life should look like.

And in a literal sense, you've achieved that.

There is no script here.

But the absence of a script doesn't eliminate direction.

It transfers it.

To you.

That's where the weight begins.

Because without a default path, every decision becomes more visible. More deliberate. You can't attribute your choices to momentum, or expectation, or necessity in the same way you once could. Even inaction becomes a kind of action, something you've allowed, something you've chosen by not choosing otherwise.

There's no neutral position.

Everything reflects back on you.

And that reflection is difficult to avoid.

You start to notice how often you hesitate, not because you don't have options, but because you have too many. Each one represents a different version of your life, a different direction, a different outcome that can't be fully predicted or reversed.

Choice expands possibility.

But it also expands consequence.

That's the part that isn't obvious at first.

When options are limited, decisions feel constrained, but also lighter. You operate within boundaries that reduce uncertainty. The path may not be entirely yours, but it's clear enough to follow without constant evaluation.

Without those boundaries, clarity has to come from within.

And that's harder to maintain.

Because internal clarity isn't fixed.

It shifts.

What feels right one moment can feel uncertain the next. What seems like a clear direction can dissolve under closer examination. You question not just your options, but the basis on which you're choosing between them.

What do I actually want?

And more importantly:

Can I trust that answer?

That's where the weight deepens.

Not in the decisions themselves, but in the responsibility behind them. The understanding that whatever direction you take isn't just something that happens, it's something you've defined.

Or failed to define.

Because even drifting, at this point, becomes a form of choice.

You're no longer unaware of it. You can't tell yourself that things are simply unfolding. You've seen how easily direction can be lost, how subtly it can be replaced by habit, by environment, by inertia.

So if you continue drifting, it's not accidental.

It's allowed.

And that awareness removes a kind of comfort.

There's no external structure to push against, no system to blame, no expectation to resist. Whatever shape your life takes, it's increasingly difficult to separate it from your own decisions, both active and passive.

You are responsible.

Not in a punitive sense.

But in a fundamental one.

For defining what your life is.

That's the part that makes freedom feel heavier than it did at the beginning.

Because now it's no longer just about escaping constraints.

It's about creating something in their absence.

And creation requires commitment.

To a direction.

To a version of yourself.

To a set of choices that inevitably close off other possibilities.

That's the hidden cost of choice.

Not just what you gain, but what you give up.

Every decision narrows the field, shaping your life in one direction while eliminating others. And when you're aware of that, fully aware, it becomes harder to move forward casually.

You feel the weight of what isn't chosen.

Not as regret, but as awareness.

That this could have been different.

That it still could be, if you were willing to choose differently.

And yet, at some point, movement becomes necessary.

You can't stay in possibility forever.

Because a life defined only by options isn't a life that's being lived.

It's one that's being considered.

So you move.

Not with certainty, but with intention.

Accepting that clarity may never be complete. That choices will always involve some degree of doubt, some awareness of what's being left behind.

And that the responsibility doesn't go away once the decision is made.

It continues.

In how you follow through.

In how you define what that choice means over time.

That's the final shift.

When choice stops being about selecting from available paths…

and becomes about creating the path itself.

And carrying the weight of it.

Fully.

Because there's no one else to carry it for you.

Epilogue: No Final Answers

It doesn't resolve.

That's the part that becomes clear in the end.

There's no moment where everything aligns, where the contradictions settle into something clean, something coherent, something you can step back from and understand completely. No final insight that ties everything together, no conclusion that transforms uncertainty into clarity.

Instead, what remains is… everything.

All of it.

The movement and the stillness. The freedom and the weight. The connection and the distance. The person you were, the person you've become, and the versions of yourself that don't fully reconcile with either.

They don't cancel each other out.

They coexist.

For a long time, you expect resolution.

You assume that if you keep going, keep thinking, reflecting, adjusting, something will eventually click into place. That the contradictions you've been navigating will resolve into a clearer understanding. That the tension you feel between different parts of your experience will ease into something more stable.

But it doesn't happen that way.

Because the contradictions aren't temporary.

They're structural.

They come from seeing more than one perspective at once. From understanding that different ways of living, thinking, and being can all feel valid, depending on where you stand.

And once you see that, you can't return to a single, unified view.

You don't simplify.

You expand.

And expansion doesn't reduce complexity.

It increases it.

That's what makes this ending different from what you might have expected.

There's no final answer to arrive at.

No definitive version of life that resolves everything that came before.

Just a growing awareness that resolution itself may have been the wrong goal.

Because life, as it actually unfolds, doesn't offer closure in the way you imagined.

It continues.

With questions that don't fully resolve.

With choices that don't guarantee clarity.

With identities that remain in motion, shaped by context, by time, by the ongoing process of living.

And somewhere along the way, that stops feeling like a problem.

Not because the ambiguity disappears, but because your relationship to it changes.

You stop needing everything to fit.

To make sense in a complete, consistent way.

You stop expecting a final version of yourself, a final understanding, a final place where everything settles and stays.

Instead, you begin to accept something quieter.

That uncertainty isn't a phase.

It's part of the structure.

That ambiguity isn't something to eliminate.

It's something to live within.

And that acceptance doesn't feel like giving up.

It feels like releasing something.

The need for resolution.

The expectation that life should arrive somewhere definitive.

Once that expectation loosens, something else becomes possible.

You can move without needing to know exactly where you're going.

You can choose without requiring certainty.

You can exist within contradiction without forcing it into alignment.

Not because you've solved anything.

But because you've stopped trying to solve everything.

That's where the book ends.

Not with an answer.

But with a recognition.

That the search for clarity, for identity, for belonging, for something stable and final, was never about reaching a conclusion.

It was about understanding the nature of the search itself.

And realizing that it doesn't end.

It just changes form.

Life continues.

Not resolved.

Not complete.

But ongoing.

And for the first time, that feels like enough.

www.ingramcontent.com/pod-product-compliance
Lightning Source LLC
Chambersburg PA
CBHW071350150726
47997CB00002B/924